2.0   147 917

Dear Parent:
Your child's love of reading starts here!

Every child learns to read in a different way and at his or her own speed. Some go back and forth between reading levels and read favorite books again and again. Others read through each level in order. You can help your young reader improve and become more confident by encouraging his or her own interests and abilities. From books your child reads with you to the first books he or she reads alone, there are I Can Read Books for every stage of reading:

SHARED READING
Basic language, word repetition, and whimsical illustrations, ideal for sharing with your emergent reader

BEGINNING READING
Short sentences, familiar words, and simple concepts for children eager to read on their own

READING WITH HELP
Engaging stories, longer sentences, and language play for developing readers

READING ALONE
Complex plots, challenging vocabulary, and high-interest topics for the independent reader

ADVANCED READING
Short paragraphs, chapters, and exciting themes for the perfect bridge to chapter books

I Can Read Books have introduced children to the joy of reading since 1957. Featuring award-winning authors and illustrators and a fabulous cast of beloved characters, I Can Read Books set the standard for beginning readers.

A lifetime of discovery begins with the magical words **"I Can Read!"**

Visit www.icanread.com for information
on enriching your child's reading experience.

For Roger & Sumaya—best buds
—H. P.

To all my old and new best friends
—L. A.

❋ ❋ ❋

I Can Read Book® is a trademark of HarperCollins Publishers.
Amelia Bedelia is a registered trademark of Peppermint Partners, LLC.

Amelia Bedelia Makes a Friend. Text copyright © 2011 by Herman S. Parish III. Illustrations copyright © 2011 by Lynne Avril. All rights reserved. No part of this book may be used or reproduced in any manner whatsoever without written permission except in the case of brief quotations embodied in critical articles and reviews. Printed in the United States of America. Gouache and black pencil were used to prepare the full-color art. For information address HarperCollins Children's Books, a division of HarperCollins Publishers, 10 East 53rd Street, New York, NY 10022.

www.icanread.com

Library of Congress Cataloging-in-Publication Data
Parish, Herman.
Amelia Bedelia makes a friend / by Herman Parish ; pictures by Lynne Avril.
    p. cm. — (I can read! 1 beginning reading)
Summary: When her best friend moves out of the house next door, Amelia Bedelia wonders who the new neighbors will be.
ISBN 978-0-06-207516-1 (trade ed.) — ISBN 978-0-06-207515-4 (pbk. ed.) [1. Best friends—Fiction. 2. Friendship—Fiction.
3. Neighbors—Fiction.] I. Avril, Lynne, ill. II. Title.   PZ7.P2185Ap 2012   [E]—dc23   2011018415

11 12 13 14 15 LP/WOR 10 9 8 7 6 5 4 3 2 1 First Edition
Greenwillow Books

Amelia Bedelia

·Makes a Friend·

by Herman Parish ❀ pictures by Lynne Avril

Greenwillow Books, *An Imprint of* HarperCollins*Publishers*

Amelia Bedelia was lucky.

Her best friend lived next door.

"Hello, Jen!" said Amelia Bedelia.

"Hi, Amelia Bedelia!" said Jen.

Amelia Bedelia and Jen

had been friends

since they were babies.

They baked together.

SALE !!!
Fresh. Mud
PIES

They dressed up together.

They played music together.

Amelia Bedelia even showed Jen
how to bowl.

"They play so well together,"
said Amelia Bedelia's mother.
"They sure do," said Jen's mother.
"Even though they are
as different as night and day."

Then one day,

Jen and her parents

moved away.

Amelia Bedelia and her parents

were very sad.

Amelia Bedelia missed Jen.

She missed Jen every day.

She wished Jen would come back.

One morning, a moving van pulled up.

"Did Jen come back?"

asked Amelia Bedelia.

"I don't think so,"

said Amelia Bedelia's mother.

"We must have new neighbors."

Amelia Bedelia's mother
watched the movers.
"Oh, look," she said.
"I see a fancy footstool."

Amelia Bedelia did not look.
She wanted Jen back.

"Look!" said Amelia Bedelia's mother.

"I see a coffee table."

Amelia Bedelia still did not look.

She just kept drawing.

Amelia Bedelia's
mother said,
"I see some
big armchairs."

"I see a loveseat."

"I see a twin bed."

Finally, Amelia Bedelia looked
at Jen's old house.

Then she looked at her drawings.

"Our new neighbors sound strange,"
she said.

That night, Amelia Bedelia

told her dad

about the new neighbors.

He loved her pictures.

"Amazing!" her dad said.

"I hope they have a pool table."

The next morning,
Amelia Bedelia and her mother
baked blueberry muffins.

They took the muffins
next door.

A lady opened the door.

"Hello there," she said.

"My name is Mrs. Adams.

You must be my new neighbors."

21

"No," said Amelia Bedelia.

"We already live here.

You are my new neighbor."

"You know," said Mrs. Adams,

"I think both of us are right.

Do come in."

"Mmmm," Mrs. Adams said.

"What smells so good?"

"My mom does," said Amelia Bedelia.

"I don't wear perfume yet."

24

Jen's house looked different.

Every room was full of boxes.

"Welcome to my mess,"

said Mrs. Adams.

"I will live out of boxes for a while."

That sounded fun to Amelia Bedelia.

"Are the twins in their bed?"

asked Amelia Bedelia.

"My goodness," said Mrs. Adams.

"You have sharp eyes."

Amelia Bedelia hoped that was good.

"My twin grandchildren

will visit today," said Mrs. Adams.

"Their names are Mary and Marty."

The twins visited that afternoon.

"Our grandma is a lot of fun,"

they told Amelia Bedelia.

They were right!

It was great to have a friend

right next door again.

Amelia Bedelia and Mrs. Adams
baked together.

They dressed up together.

They played music together.

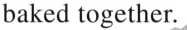

"They have so much fun together,"
said Amelia Bedelia's father.
"They sure do,"
said Amelia Bedelia's mother.
"Even though they are
as different as night and day."

One day Jen came back to visit.

Mrs. Adams took both girls

to a real bowling alley.

"This is the best day ever,"

said Amelia Bedelia.

"I have a best old friend

and a best new friend.

We are three best friends together!"